The Yippy, Yappy Yorkie
in the Green Doggy Sweater

By Debbie Macomber & Mary Lou Carney

Illustrations by Sally Anne Lambert

HARPER

An Imprint of HarperCollinsPublishers

Also by Debbie Macomber & Mary Lou Carney
The Truly Terribly Horrible Sweater . . . That Grandma Knit

The Yippy, Yappy Yorkie in the Green Doggy Sweater
Text copyright © 2012 by Debbie Macomber and Mary Lou Carney
Illustrations copyright © 2012 by Sally Anne Lambert
All rights reserved. Manufactured in China.
No part of this book may be used or reproduced in any manner whatsoever without written permission except
in the case of brief quotations embodied in critical articles and reviews. For information address HarperCollins
Children's Books, a division of HarperCollins Publishers, 10 East 53rd Street, New York, NY 10022.
www.harpercollinschildren.com

Library of Congress Cataloging-in-Publication Data
Macomber, Debbie.
The yippy, yappy Yorkie in the green doggy sweater / by Debbie Macomber &
Mary Lou Carney ; illustrations by Sally Anne Lambert. — 1st ed.
p.   cm. — (A Blossom Street kids book)
Summary: Ellen moves with her mother and her Yorkie named Baxter to a new neighborhood where
before too long Ellen is pleased to feel right at home with some unexpected help from Baxter.
ISBN 978-0-06-165096-3 (trade bdg.) — ISBN 978-0-06-165097-0 (lib. bdg.)
[1. Moving, Household—Fiction.   2. Neighborhoods—Fiction.   3. Yorkshire terrier—Fiction.
4. Dogs—Fiction.]   I. Carney, Mary Lou.   II. Lambert, Sally Anne, ill.   III. Title.
PZ7.M241Yi 2012   [E]—dc22   2010017941   CIP   AC

Typography by Rachel Zegar
12 13 14 15 16   SCP   10 9 8 7 6 5 4 3 2 1
❖
First Edition

It was moving day on Blossom Street. And Ellen wasn't sure Baxter was happy about it. Ellen wasn't sure she was happy about it either.

Ellen scooped Baxter up. Together they looked out the window. She could see the bright awning of Susannah's Garden, the flower shop on the corner. Alix, at the French Café, was putting fresh cakes into the big display window. Down the street was A Good Yarn, where Ellen had learned to knit. She'd even knit Baxter his very own sweater.

"I don't want to move either," she whispered into Baxter's ear.
"But Mom says I'll make new friends. I'll have a big room, and you'll
have a backyard to run and play in."

Baxter wiggled out of Ellen's arms and jumped down. He began running in circles, yipping and yapping as he chased his tail. "You're so silly!" She laughed.

"Ellen," Mom called from the kitchen. "Are you finished packing?" "Almost!" Ellen answered.

"Baxter, would you like to wear your sweater?" Ellen was proud that she had knit Baxter's sweater—it hadn't been easy to do. Baxter stood extra still as Ellen slipped on the bright green sweater.

"Don't you look handsome!" Ellen said. Baxter just yipped
and yapped some more.

The new house was just as lovely as her mother had said it would be. Only it wasn't like the one on Blossom Street.

Her new bedroom was big, with two windows, but it wasn't like her bedroom at home. "I like my old bedroom better. I don't care that it was small."

Mom placed her arm around Ellen's shoulders. "You'll like this one too. And Baxter has a place to play in the sun." Baxter yipped and yapped and looked out the window. "See? Baxter can't wait to go outside!"

Ellen began unpacking while Mom let Baxter
outside to explore the backyard.

When she had finished lining up
her books on the shelf, Ellen looked
out the window and saw Baxter
chasing a butterfly.

The next time she looked, he was asleep under a lilac bush.

When all her clothes were
hanging in her closet,

and all her stuffed animals were
sitting in a row on her bed,

and all her pajamas and T-shirts
were tucked into drawers,

Ellen decided to show Baxter how nice her room looked.

She opened the back door and called, "Baxter! Baxter!"
But the backyard was empty.
Ellen called his name over and over. "Baxter! Baxter!"

She looked under the lilac bush and in the vegetable garden too. That was when she found a hole in the fence. A little hole just big enough for a yippy, yappy Yorkie. And there was a piece of green yarn caught on the wood!

"Mom! Mom!" Ellen said, racing inside. "Baxter is gone! We have to find him!"

Soon Ellen and her mother
were walking through their new
neighborhood, looking for Baxter.
    They came to a man standing
beside a bright yellow truck just
like the one in the park off Blossom
Street. He was selling ice cream.

"Have you seen a yippy, yappy Yorkie in a green doggy sweater?" Ellen asked.

"No," the man replied. "But I have seen lots of Popsicles and ice-cream sandwiches and Eskimo pies!"

Next they came to a grocery store a lot like the one on Blossom Street. A man in a long striped apron was stacking fruit in tall piles. "Have you seen a yippy, yappy Yorkie in a green doggy sweater?"

"No," the man said, beginning to juggle an apple, a peach, and an orange. "But I have seen watermelons and bananas and kiwi!"

Up ahead, a woman was washing a window. Big letters spelled
out BRENDA'S BAKERY. Ellen could smell all the wonderful things baking
inside. They smelled just as yummy as the goodies at the French Café.

"Have you seen a yippy, yappy Yorkie in a green doggy sweater?"
The woman stopped wiping and smiled. "No, but I have seen doughnuts and crème puffs and oatmeal raisin cookies!"

"Oh, Mom!" Ellen cried. "What if we never find Baxter?"

"Let's keep looking," her mother said. "He can't have gone far on those short little legs!"

At the end of the street was a flower shop just like Susannah's Garden on Blossom Street. Big buckets of spring flowers sat on the sidewalk. There was a pink awning over the door.

"Maybe Baxter is there!" Ellen said. She rushed inside. "Have you seen a yippy, yappy Yorkie—"

But before she could even finish her question, a girl about the same age as Ellen answered, "Yes! In fact, I've seen two of them!" and pointed.

Inside the store, there was Baxter, playing with another dog.

"Baxter!" Ellen said, kneeling down and lifting him into her arms. "I was so worried!"

Baxter yipped and yapped and licked her face.

"Thank you for keeping him safe," Mom said.

"I figured someone would come looking for him soon," the girl
said. She bent down to pet her own Yorkie. "Besides, my dog, Iris, has
a new friend now! I love his green doggy sweater."

"I knit it!" Ellen said, still hugging Baxter.

"I'm April. Can you teach me to knit?"

Ellen smiled and nodded.

As they walked back home with Baxter on his leash, Ellen said to Mom, "Our new neighborhood is a lot like Blossom Street."

"Yes, it is. There are friends here too. Friends just waiting for you to meet them!"

When they got home, Ellen went up to her bedroom and looked around. It really was nice, with plenty of space to invite her new friends over. She'd invite April first and teach her how to knit.

And before long, Ellen and April were walking
around the neighborhood, showing

the ice-cream man

and the grocer

and the baker

and anyone else who wanted to look

TWO yippy, yappy Yorkies
     in green doggy sweaters.